Bird Bonanza

Don't miss a single

Nancy Drew
Clue Book:

Nancy Drew
* CLUE BOOK *

#18

Bird Bonanza

BY CAROLYN KEENE * ILLUSTRATED BY PETER FRANCIS

Aladdin
NEW YORK   LONDON   TORONTO   SYDNEY   NEW DELHI

ALADDIN

An imprint of Simon & Schuster Children's Publishing Division
1230 Avenue of the Americas, New York, New York 10020
First Aladdin hardcover edition June 2023
Text copyright © 2023 by Simon & Schuster, Inc.
Illustrations copyright © 2023 by Peter Francis
Also available in an Aladdin paperback edition.
ALADDIN and related logo are registered trademarks of Simon & Schuster, Inc.
NANCY DREW, NANCY DREW CLUEBOOK, and colophons
are registered trademarks of Simon & Schuster, Inc.
All rights reserved, including the right of reproduction in whole or in part in any form.
For information about special discounts for bulk purchases, please contact Simon & Schuster
Special Sales at 1-866-506-1949 or business@simonandschuster.com.
The Simon & Schuster Speakers Bureau can bring authors to your live event.
For more information or to book an event contact the Simon & Schuster Speakers Bureau
at 1-866-248-3049 or visit our website at www.simonspeakers.com.
Series designed by Karina Granda
Interior designed by Tom Daly
The illustrations for this book were rendered digitally.
The text of this book was set in Adobe Garamond Pro.
Manufactured in the United States of America 0423 OFF
2 4 6 8 10 9 7 5 3 1
Library of Congress Cataloging-in-Publication Data
Names: Keene, Carolyn, author. | Francis, Peter, 1973– illustrator.
Title: Bird bonanza / by Carolyn Keene ; illustrated by Peter Francis.
Description: First Aladdin hardcover/paperback edition. | New York :
Aladdin, 2023. | Series: Nancy Drew clue book ; 18 | Audience: Ages 6 to 9. |
Summary: The Clue Crew investigates who sabotaged the River Heights Nature Park's fundraiser.
Identifiers: LCCN 2022054546 (print) | LCCN 2022054547 (ebook) |
ISBN 9781534488243 (paperback) | ISBN 9781534488250 (hardcover) |
ISBN 9781534488267 (ebook)
Subjects: CYAC: Mystery and detective stories. | Natural areas—Fiction. |
Fund raising—Fiction. | Sabotage—Fiction. | Birds—Fiction. | BISAC:
JUVENILE FICTION / Mysteries & Detective Stories | JUVENILE FICTION /
Readers / Chapter Books | LCGFT: Detective and mystery fiction. | Novels.
Classification: LCC PZ7.K23 Bj 2023 (print) | LCC PZ7.K23 (ebook) | DDC
[Fic]—dc23
L
LC e

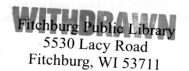

* CONTENTS *

Bird Bonanza

Chapter

SWAG BAG SNAG

"I'm a Bluebird," Nancy announced. It was the first day of Bird Bonanza Camp at the River Heights Nature Park. Nancy had found her name on the list at the sign-in table in the Welcome Center. Next, she ran her finger down the page, looking for BESS MARVIN and GEORGE FAYNE, her two best friends. "We're all on Team Bluebird," Nancy reported happily. Bess and George squealed with delight.

"Here's the plan," said George. She whipped

a calculator out of her back pocket. "If we each learn to identify five new birds per day . . . That's five times three . . ." She stuck out her tongue as she punched the numbers on the keypad.

"We know you want to win the Big Bird Count raffle prize," Bess said, narrowing her eyes at George. The girls were cousins as well as friends. "But I'm here for bird-watching, not bird-counting."

"The top prize in the big count is a pair of PowerTron 5000s," George gushed. "You can practically see to the moon with binoculars that strong. I have to win!" George had a pile of electronic gadgets at home, but she could never get enough.

"It's not a contest," Nancy reminded her. "It's a raffle. Everyone who participates in the Big Bird Count gets their name entered. You have as good a chance as anyone to win."

George groaned. "But I don't know the names of many birds. You have to know what the birds are called for your numbers to count."

"That's what Bird Bonanza Camp is for." Bess held up a small bird guide she had tucked in the outside pocket of her lunch cooler. She liked to be super prepared for every adventure. "Nancy and I will quiz you. We'll describe a bird, and you can guess what kind it is."

"We'll all learn together." Nancy's blue eyes twinkled.

"That plan is for the birds—in a good way." George grinned.

"Let's go grab our swag bags," suggested Bess. She pointed to a swarm of campers crowded around a table on the other side of the room. The kids were all wearing baseball caps in different colors—red, orange, yellow, and black. "I think our team hats are in those bags."

As the girls made their way over to the swag bag station, three black-capped Chickadees moved away, and Nancy, Bess, and George took their spots. The table was piled high with Bird Bonanza backpacks, each with a camper's name on it.

"I found mine," said Nancy. She pulled out a blue cap and placed it on her head, over her reddish-blond hair. Then she stowed her lunch bag inside her new backpack.

"I can't find mine," George complained.

"Do I need the Clue Book?" Nancy asked. She patted her back pocket where she kept the special notebook she shared with her friends. They used it to write down suspects and clues when they had a big mystery to solve. The third-graders were the best detectives at River Heights Elementary School. They'd even formed a club called the Clue Crew.

"Mystery solved. I found it," Bess called. Her blond waves peeked out from under her blue hat as she handed the bag to her cousin. "They wrote your real name on it—*Georgia*." Bess smirked. She knew how much George hated her real name.

"No one better call me that. That's all I have to say," George grumbled as she yanked her cap sideways on top of her dark curls. She and her

cousin put their lunch bags in their new swag bags and zipped them up.

A boy squeezed into the crowd next to Nancy. He wore black pants, a white collared shirt, a top hat, shiny shoes, and a red magician's cape—not exactly the best outfit for spending a day outdoors.

"Hey, Jason," another boy on the opposite side of the table called out. "Where have you been? I've been looking everywhere for you."

"I've been around. What did you think, Peter? That I did my famous disappearing act?"

Peter shrugged.

Jason had already grabbed his swag bag. He unzipped it and Nancy could see that he'd stashed his lunch bag inside. Jason frowned. "There's nothing fun in here," he griped. "Just a dumb hat, a trail map, and . . . What's this?" He held up a piece of paper that had been rolled up like a scroll.

"It's our list of activities," Peter explained as he unrolled and read his own sheet of paper. "It looks like we have a birdsong workshop first, then a hike to do some bird-watching at Turkey Trench. Bird Bonanza Camp is going to be awesome!"

"I can't believe Mom made us go to nature camp," Jason complained. "At magician camp, they give out magic wands." He shoved the blue cap on his head, then placed his top hat carefully in the bag on top of his lunch.

"Mom didn't *make* us go to nature camp. I *wanted* to go, remember? And I won the coin toss, so I got to choose." Unlike his brother, Peter was dressed for the outdoors. Nancy noticed he also wore a blue baseball cap.

Nancy, Bess, and George shot one another quizzical looks. It was obvious from their hats that the brothers were on Team Bluebird too. Nancy could tell what her friends were thinking: *We're not going to have to listen to these guys squabble all week, are we?*

Just then, a young woman with short dark curly hair and a kind smile approached them. She was wearing cargo pants with deep pockets, and a pair of binoculars hung around her neck. "There you are, Bluebirds. My name is Lauren, and I'm your team leader." She checked her clipboard. "There are five of you on my list, and I see five blue hats. Would you please tell me your names?"

"I'm Nancy, and these are my best friends, Bess and George." Bess smiled, and George gave a quick wave.

"I'm Peter, and this is my brother, Jason."

"You can call me Mr. Magic," Jason added. "Everyone does."

Peter scowled at his brother. "No one calls you Mr. Magic. You just *want* people to call you that."

Jason stuck out his tongue.

"Welcome to Bird Bonanza Camp," Lauren said, ignoring the sibling spat. "We have tons of fun planned and—"

"Aaaahhh!" Bess shrieked, tossing her backpack on the floor. "Help! It's a snake!"

George kneeled by Bess's bag and peeked inside, then giggled. "You dodo. It's made of rubber. See?"

Bess reached in and carefully touched the object that had given her such a bad scare. "A fake snake? Who put that in my bag?"

"I did," Jason crowed. "Pretty good trick, right? You didn't even see me do it."

"That's not funny," said Bess, crossing her arms.

"Or nice," Nancy added.

George chuckled. "Maybe it was a *little* funny."

"Whose side are you on?" Bess asked, pouting at her cousin.

Lauren cleared her throat to get the group's attention. "Loud noises scare the birds away, Bluebirds, so no more tricks or pranks, especially outdoors. Okay, Jason?"

"Okay, no more tricks," he promised.

"*For now*," Nancy heard him mutter softly.

Chapter

2

TWEET TALK

"It's time for our birdsong workshop, Bluebirds," Lauren sang cheerfully. "Follow me, please." She made her way across the room toward the Welcome Center exit.

Jason tugged his brother's T-shirt. "Hey, Peter, speaking of blue, what's red and smells like blue paint?"

"I don't know," Peter grumbled, without giving his brother a glance.

"Red paint!" Jason laughed at his own joke.

Bess and Nancy giggled, and George broke into a wide smile. "That's a pretty good one," she said.

As Nancy followed her group through the doorway, a woman wearing a wide-brimmed hat hurried past her in the opposite direction. Surprised, Nancy let the door go too soon, and it hit the woman on the back of her leg. "Oops! Sorry!" she called, but the woman didn't reply and didn't stop.

With a shrug, Nancy rushed to catch up to the rest of Team Bluebird, who'd formed a line behind Lauren and were following her across a grassy field.

"We're like ducks in a row," Bess pointed out. George and Nancy giggled.

Jason flapped his cape. "Quack, quack!"

His brother frowned. "Jason, you don't have to be the center of attention every single minute."

"I do if I'm going to be a famous magician someday," Jason shot back. Peter rolled his eyes.

Once they'd reached a shady spot beneath a maple tree, Lauren stopped, spreading her arms and gesturing to the ground. "Everyone, find a comfortable seat," she said. Nancy and her friends sat cross-legged on the soft grass. Peter and Jason found a spot on a log.

Off in the distance, a bird trilled, *Chickadee-dee-dee.*

"Do you hear that?" Lauren asked. "Do you know what type of bird it is?"

"It's a Carolina chickadee," Peter answered.

"That's right," said Lauren. "Very good."

"What does it look like?" asked George. "I need to learn how to identify birds to get ready for the Big Bird Count."

Just then, a pair of small gray-and-black birds swooped overhead and landed on a low branch nearby. "There they are," Peter said, pointing to the birds.

Chickadee-dee-dee.

"They have a pretty song," Bess remarked after a moment.

"Why do I get the feeling that they're mad at us?" asked Nancy.

Lauren laughed. "They are a little mad. We're too close to their feeder. Chickadees do not like intruders. They're warning us away. I'll give them extra seeds to make them feel better." Lauren pulled a small paper bag from her pocket, walked over to a feeder, and tipped the bag into the opening. A handful of seeds spilled onto the ground, and a small gray squirrel grabbed some before darting away.

Next, Lauren took an orange out of her pocket, sliced it in half using a pocketknife, and placed the halves in the feeder alongside the seeds.

"Why did you give the birds an orange?" George asked.

"I know why," Peter piped up. "Birds fly for miles and miles until they find the perfect spot to build their nests. Oranges give birds extra nutrition and energy."

Lauren smiled at him. "That's right, Peter. You already seem to know a lot about birds."

"I want to be an ornithologist when I grow up. I love learning about birds," Peter said.

"Then I think you'll like my next surprise. I have something for each of you." Lauren pulled bird whistles out of her vest pocket and handed one to each camper. "These are for you to keep."

"We're actually going to *talk* to the birds?" George asked.

"Don't be silly. That's impossible." Bess shook her head.

The corners of George's eyes crinkled with annoyance. "Me, silly? At least I'm not afraid of a rubber snake."

"Hey! Don't rub it in!"

"It's not only possible to communicate with birds, it's fun," Lauren said before the cousins could continue arguing. "If you tweet a bird's special song, they often tweet back. I'll show you."

Lauren blew *tweet tweet tweet* with her whistle. "Now you try."

Together, the campers blew *tweet tweet tweet*.

A bird perched in a nearby pine tree whistled back *tweet, tweet, tweet*.

"Look, it's a robin," said George. She pointed

to the gray bird with the red belly. "That's one I already know."

"Amazing," Nancy cooed. She smiled at the robin as it bobbed its neck left and right, like it had a question.

Jason gazed up at the bird. "That's a pretty cool trick," he admitted reluctantly. Then a smile spread across his face. "Hey, I think I know what that robin wants to ask us. What's brown and sticky?" He didn't wait for a response before he called out, "A stick!" He clutched his sides with glee. "Wait, wait! I've got another one—how do you know when you see a dogwood tree? By its bark!"

Nancy, George, and Bess chuckled, but Peter groaned. "Your jokes are for the birds, Jason." He leaped to his feet and looked up at the blue sky dotted with fluffy clouds. "Lauren, do you think we could call an eagle? I've always wanted to see one."

Lauren gave a half shrug. "I'm afraid I wouldn't get my hopes up, Peter. Eagles are beautiful birds, but sightings are pretty rare."

Peter nodded, disappointed, then dropped slowly back to his seat.

"Let's learn another one," Bess suggested. Nancy and George nodded in agreement.

"How about a cardinal—" Lauren was saying when a woman approached the Bluebirds from the direction of the Welcome Center. She had soft gray curls and wore a nature park uniform. Nancy thought she seemed familiar.

"There you are, Lauren," the woman called out. "I've been looking for you." Behind her trailed a young brown-haired girl wearing green shorts and a yellow shirt with a bright purple butterfly on the front. Her eyes were red and she was sniffling. Nancy felt bad for the girl, who was clearly upset about something.

"Hello, Dr. Giblet," said Lauren.

"Oh, I'm so glad I caught up with you." The woman seemed friendly, but Nancy thought she looked worried. "Hello, everyone. I'm Dr. Hazel Giblet. I'm the River Heights Nature Park's director. And this is Tessa." She placed her hand on the girl's shoulder. "Mr. Hebert's granddaughter."

"Mr. Hebert, the head groundskeeper?" asked Lauren.

"That's right," said Dr. Giblet. "Tessa was supposed to spend the day with him, but he's terribly busy getting the grounds ready for the Big Bird Count. Could she join your group?"

"Of course."

Tessa wiped her eyes and nose with a wad of tissues from her pocket. "Thank you," she said. "Grandpa and I were supposed to go butterfly-watching today, but now he can't." Her shoulders slumped.

"While we look for birds, you can look for butterflies. How does that sound?" Lauren asked.

"Okay, I guess."

"I'd better be off," said Dr. Giblet. "There's been a disaster in the greenhouse."

Nancy's ears perked up. To the members of

the Clue Crew, "disaster" was just another word for "mystery." "What happened?" she asked.

"Someone broke into the greenhouse and destroyed the flowers and shrubs we'd planned to sell at the plant sale on Big Bird Count Day. The place is a mess. There are broken pots and smooshed petals everywhere."

"What's the plant sale for?" asked Bess.

"We were going to sell bird-friendly plants to park visitors on Big Bird Count Day to raise money for the nature park. The funds help us buy things we need for the animals who live at the nature park, like birdseed for our feeders. But unfortunately, now the plants are ruined."

"Oh no," said Lauren, shaking her head.

"And that's not all," Dr. Giblet continued. "The raffle prize has gone missing."

George gasped and her eyes went wide. "Not the PowerTron 5000s! What happened?"

"They were in the greenhouse for safekeeping," Dr. Giblet replied, "but they've vanished. And I'm not sure it would be fair to hold the Big Bird

Count without the prize we promised. I may have to cancel the event."

Peter's hands flew to his cheeks. "You can't cancel the Big Bird Count!"

"That would be terrible," Jason said. Nancy heard him mumble "not" under his breath.

"Try not to worry," said Dr. Giblet. "It might not come to that. The raffle prize could still turn up. I'd better run now, though. Have a good day, Team Bluebird, and try to enjoy yourself, Tessa." With that, Dr. Giblet darted back toward the Welcome Center.

"What's the big deal about the Big Bird Count, anyway?" Jason mumbled.

"It's only the biggest birding event of the year," Peter explained. "Volunteers come from all over to find all the different types of birds that live here. Songbirds, warblers, finches . . . you name it!"

Nancy's brow furrowed. "Why do they do that?"

"Counting birds helps scientists learn where healthy groups of birds live," Peter told them. "If they see numbers going down, they can figure out places where birds might be in danger and figure out what changed. Right, Lauren?"

"That's right. The purpose of the count is to make sure birds have safe habitats." Lauren frowned. "It would be a shame if Dr. Giblet had to cancel the event."

"Without the PowerTron 5000s, it looks like the Big Bird Count is kaput," Jason remarked. "Tessa, you might be able to go butterfly-catching with your grandpa after all."

"Not catching," she corrected. "Catching butterflies can hurt them. We just watch them. They're so pretty."

"Okay, so if Big Bird Count Day is canceled, you could go chase butterflies." He turned to Peter. "Let's tell Mom we want to switch to magician camp. Maybe then *I* can get my magic wand."

Chapter

TRAGIC MAGIC

"There has to be a way to save the Big Bird Count," said Peter.

"And find those binoculars," George added.

Nancy grinned. "This sounds like a job for the Clue Crew."

"The Clue Crew?" Lauren looked confused.

"That's the name of our club," George explained.

"We're detectives," said Bess. "Solving mysteries is what we do."

Nancy stood up and brushed herself off, then

narrowed her eyes. George and Bess could tell that she was hatching a plan. "Lauren, would you please take us to see the greenhouse right away?"

Lauren frowned. "I'm not sure that's a good idea. If it's as big a disaster as Dr. Giblet says, we'd better stay out of the way."

"The early bird catches the worm," George replied. "The sooner we get there, the sooner we can figure out what happened."

"If the early bird catches the worm, I'll wait until later for the pancakes," Jason said.

"Knock off the jokes already," Peter grumbled.

Jason grinned. "You want a knock-knock joke?"

"Stop! Why can't you ever be serious?"

Jason turned to the others. "My brother is always bossing me around. He told me to stop acting like a flamingo once, so I had to put my foot down."

Peter groaned and dropped his head into his hands.

Nancy thought Jason's joke was pretty funny, but they had a case to focus on. "We won't get in the way, Lauren," she promised.

"Maybe we can help sweep up the dirt," Bess offered. She usually liked to keep her clothes crisp and clean, but mysteries were worth getting a little messy for.

"And my grandpa might be at the greenhouse working," added Tessa. "I could visit with him after all."

Lauren looked uncertain. "Bird Camp is supposed to be about exploring the outdoors. Are you sure this is what you want to do?"

Peter perked up. "It is if we can save the Big Bird Count, right, Jason?"

"Can I practice magic tricks?"

"No," Peter said, giving his brother an annoyed look.

"Then it doesn't matter what I think. I'll come to the greenhouse if you want me to."

"Please?" Nancy begged.

Lauren sighed. "All right. You win. Come on." Team Bluebird followed her to a short path behind the Welcome Center. When they reached the greenhouse, Lauren pulled out a key and unlocked the front door.

"It is *hot* in here now," Jason complained.

"What do you mean 'now'?" asked Peter. "Have you been here before?"

"Um, no. That's not what I meant. I just mean I'm hot right *now*." Jason fanned his face with his cape.

"It smells like perfume," Bess said, clapping

her hands. She gazed at the rows of leafy plants with red, yellow, and purple blossoms.

Nancy took a few cautious steps forward, looking around the space. "Dr. Giblet was right. This place is a disaster." Broken pottery, dirt, leaves, and petals were strewn across the floor. "Lauren, do you know where the PowerTron 5000s were kept?"

"Yes, they were on that shelf over there next to Mr. Hebert's workbench," Lauren said, pointing across the room.

Nancy pulled the Clue Book out of her back pocket and clicked her ballpoint pen, ready to start scribbling notes. "This workbench?" she asked, as George and Bess picked through the mess.

"That's the one," said Lauren.

The shelf above where the PowerTron 5000s had been sitting held a wooden box with torn-up seed packets inside. Under the shelf was a large flowerpot filled with dirt.

"Everything around here belongs in a greenhouse," said Nancy, pointing to an empty potting soil bag on the ground. "I don't see anything that could be a clue. Do you?" she asked her friends.

George shook her head.

"Nothing seems out of place," Bess added.

"Hey, Lauren, some of these plants look all right," said Peter. "We should try to save what we can. The birds need them. Let's use the pots, soil, and spades on that bench to repot the flowers."

"Good idea." Lauren grinned. "We're going to need a broom and a dustpan, too, so we can clean up what we can't save."

"I think there's some cleanup stuff in the back," said Jason, starting to make his way toward the rear of the greenhouse.

"How do you know?" Peter demanded.

"I don't know for sure." Jason's cheeks turned pink. "It was just a guess."

"He's right," said Tessa. "My grandpa hangs the broom and dustpan on a hook by the back door."

"I'll go get them," Nancy offered. She tucked the Clue Book under her arm and grabbed Bess and George by their elbows. "Come with me," she whispered.

"Do I have to?" George complained. "You need help carrying a broom?"

"No," Nancy replied quietly. "But I do need to talk to you."

"What's going on?" asked Bess.

Nancy waited until they were at the far end of the greenhouse before she answered. "Jason's acting weird. I think he's been here before."

"That's impossible," said George, crossing her

arms. "It's the first day of camp. None of the Bluebirds have been here before."

"Tessa has," Nancy noted.

"That's different. Her grandpa works here."

"If Jason has never been here before, then how did he know where to find the broom?" Nancy asked. "And why did he say that it's hot in here 'now'?"

"He's right about that," said Bess, waving a hand in front of her face.

"There's got to be a way to open a window or something," George said. She moved to the far back corner, looking for a window latch. Suddenly, she felt a cool breeze coming from overhead. "Look!" She pointed to a small, screen-covered opening in the ceiling where a breeze flowed in. "It's *much* cooler over here."

Bess joined her cousin in the corner, and Nancy followed.

"Ah! Much better," said Bess. After a moment, she asked, "So, Nancy, do you really think Jason broke in earlier and made this mess?"

"And stole the PowerTron 5000s?" George added.

"Maybe." Nancy shrugged. "He pulled the snake prank on you this morning."

"Don't remind me," Bess grumbled.

"Maybe that's his thing—telling jokes and doing tricks and causing trouble."

"But why would Jason want to steal the raffle prize?" George asked.

"Maybe he's trying to ruin Bird Bonanza Camp so his mom will let him go to magic camp instead. Remember at the swag bag station? Peter asked Jason where he was."

"How would Jason know how to get to the greenhouse, though?" asked Bess.

"He already had his swag bag with the trail map, and the greenhouse is right behind the Welcome Center. It's not hard to find."

George nodded. "Good point."

Nancy flipped open the Clue Book. "Right now it looks like Jason is our top suspect."

"He could have come to the greenhouse earlier this morning when Peter didn't know where he was," George said. "That's opportunity."

"And he has a motive," Bess added. "He wants to go to magic camp. He thinks nature camp is for the birds—and *not* in a good way."

All three girls looked up from the Clue Book. Across the greenhouse, Lauren, Peter, and Tessa were replanting the ruined flowers, but Jason didn't seem to be helping. He had taken off his cape and draped it over a small table.

"What other clues do we have?" Nancy asked, eagerly clicking her pen.

"The front door was locked," George noted. "Lauren just used a key to open it. How would Jason have gotten in?"

"Maybe through the back door?"

Just as Nancy crossed to the space to test the knob, the back door swung open, and a gruff-looking man stepped inside. "What are you three girls doing here?" he demanded. "Campers aren't supposed to be in the greenhouse without an adult."

"We—I—we—" Bess stammered.

"We're looking for the broom and dustpan," Nancy said, rescuing her friend.

"Hi, Grandpa!" called Tessa from the other side of the greenhouse. She ran over and threw her arms around the grouchy man.

"Hello, my dear." Mr. Hebert released her from the hug and ruffled her hair. A smile transformed his angry face. "Your mother texted me that she dropped you off at the Welcome Center this morning. She said you were going to spend the day with a group of campers."

"That's us," George explained.

"We're Team Bluebird," added Bess, no longer afraid.

"Hello, Mr. Hebert," said Lauren, joining them. She turned to Nancy, Bess, and George. "Were you able to find the broom?"

"What do you need the broom for?" Mr. Hebert asked.

"Didn't Dr. Giblet tell you?"

"No." Mr. Hebert's brow furrowed. "I haven't seen Dr. Giblet all morning."

Lauren explained about the break-in and the missing prize.

"If they cancel the Big Bird Count, you and I could go look for butterflies, like you promised. Right, Grandpa?" asked Tessa. Nancy noticed her red eyes had cleared up and her sniffling had stopped.

"Sure, sweetheart, but—"

CRASH!

"Jason!" cried Peter. "What did you do?"

Chapter

4

CAPE CATASTROPHE

Nancy and the others rushed to the front of the greenhouse, where they found Jason standing in the middle of a fresh mess of broken pots and plants. Peter's face was bright red and he was still shouting at his brother.

"Are you both okay?" Lauren asked. "What happened?"

Peter buried his hands in his hair. "Jason was trying to do the tablecloth trick, but all he did was make even more of a mess!"

"What's the tablecloth trick?" asked Tessa.

"It's when you pull a tablecloth out from underneath a set of dishes. If the trick works, you can whip the tablecloth out, but the dishes all stay in place on the table," Jason explained.

Bess pressed her hands to her cheeks. "This looks more like a cape catastrophe."

"I was using my cape instead of a tablecloth, and I almost had it. Then you had to go and distract me."

"I'm trying to save the plants. You ruined them—again!" Peter fired back.

"The trick worked when I did it before. I thought it would work this time."

"What do you mean, 'this time'?" Nancy asked. "Did you already try the trick in here? Are you the one who broke in earlier?"

"And if you are, tell us where you hid the binoculars right this minute!" George demanded.

Jason took a step back. "What? No way. I haven't done anything wrong."

"Well, you wrecked those plants," Bess said,

pointing to the broken pots. "And Peter said he couldn't find you in the Welcome Center this morning."

"I don't think my brother stole anything," Peter interjected, "but I was looking for you. Where did you go?"

"I was . . . um. I—"

"Well . . . ?" Nancy tapped her foot impatiently.

"Look, it's not a secret that I thought Bird Bonanza camp would be boring. I wanted to spice things up by doing some magic tricks." Jason shrugged. "I was scouting an opening to hide my snake in someone's swag bag. You can't blame me for wanting to have a little fun. Still, it's hard to be sneaky dressed like this." Jason waved his hand from his head to his toes like a magician's assistant. "Then, when I saw someone leave the Welcome Center out the back door, it gave me an idea."

Peter folded his arms across his chest. "I'll bite. What was your big idea?"

"It's better to practice magic tricks away from

a crowd so they can't see when things go wrong." Jason glanced down at the pile of rubble.

"You can say that again," Tessa said with a shrug.

"I have a few tricks up my sleeve, and I wanted to find a private spot to practice, so when I saw the person dash out the back door, I followed her."

"You should have stayed in the Welcome Center until you checked in with Team Bluebird," Lauren said, looking disappointed. "Wandering around the park on your own isn't safe."

"I wasn't really alone. I was following someone who looked like she knew where she was going. When I got near the greenhouse, I saw all the flowers inside and thought I would pick a few to use in my top hat trick. You know, the one where a magician pulls flowers out of his hat?"

"And did you?" Nancy asked.

"Did I what?"

"Pick a few flowers," George demanded. "Or did you knock all the flowers to the ground instead *and* steal the PowerTron 5000s?"

"I didn't do *anything*. The girl I was following didn't have a backpack, so I couldn't even pull the snake prank on her anyway. I never even went inside the greenhouse. I was afraid Team Bluebird would leave without me, so I ran back to the Welcome Center."

"Then why did you say that the tablecloth trick worked *before*?" asked Nancy.

"I meant I've been practicing at home, and it worked a few times. Other times, not so much." Jason shrugged sheepishly, then crouched down to pick up his rumpled cape from the stone floor. Shaking it out, he retied it around his neck.

Peter raised his eyebrows. "That's true. Jason has broken a lot of plates. Mom and Dad said if he breaks any more, it's coming out of his allowance."

"Okay, but even if that's true, how did you know where the broom was?" asked George.

"I guessed. I didn't see it up front, so I thought it might be in the back."

"Are you sure you're not trying to get us

kicked out of Bird Bonanza Camp so you can go to magic camp?" asked Peter.

"I know you love birds as much as I love jokes and magic tricks." Jason held his hand out for a fist bump, but Peter didn't return it. "I may not like being here as much as you do, but I don't want to ruin your fun. I mean it. I promise I'll stop fooling around now. For real this time."

Peter sighed. He bumped his fist against Jason's, then they both wiggled their fingers. "Okay. I guess I believe you."

Jason smiled.

"We all believe you," said Nancy. She opened her Clue Book and crossed out Jason's name, then gave Bess and George a meaningful look. Jason was no longer their number one suspect.

"All right, kids," Mr. Hebert said, clearing his throat. "I know you're trying to help, but I think I can take it from here. I'll clean up and look for the missing raffle prize. If I find it, I'll be sure to let you know right away. In the meantime, you're supposed to be here for camp. You go have some fun."

"I want to stay here with you, Grandpa," said Tessa. Nancy noticed that Tessa seemed to be happier when she was around her grandfather.

"I think you should go with Team Bluebird for now," he replied gently.

Lauren gave Tessa a bright smile and wrapped an arm around her shoulder. "Your grandpa is right. We have lots of fun activities planned, and we should get out of his way." She checked her clipboard. "Next on the agenda is a bird-watching hike to Turkey Trench. What do you say, gang? Is it time to go talk turkey?"

Chapter

TRENCH STENCH

Team Bluebird hiked down Pinewood Path toward Turkey Trench. Along the way, Lauren stopped to place more seeds and oranges in a feeder hanging from a low branch. A pair of Carolina chickadees flew in quickly. *Chickadee-dee-dee*, they tweeted.

As she walked by, Nancy looked back to see if the birds were eating the oranges. She noticed instead that two squirrels had climbed the tree and were stealing food from the feeder. *Chickadee-dee-dee, chickadee-dee-dee, chickadee-dee dee dee,*

the chickadees squawked, but the squirrels paid them no attention. Nancy felt sorry for the birds. She wouldn't like it if pesky squirrels came and stole *her* food.

Some spots along the trail were damp and muddy. "These shoes are terrible for hiking," Jason groaned. "They're too slippery." His once-shiny shoes were covered in muck. Nancy, George, and Bess slowed their pace to walk with him. Meanwhile, Tessa chased every butterfly, dragonfly, and bumblebee along the path. Lauren and Peter walked faster to keep up with her.

"I'm sorry we accused you of messing up the greenhouse and stealing the binoculars," Nancy began.

"It's all right," Jason replied. "And it kind of makes sense, too. A lot of clues pointed to me. After I knocked all those plants over trying to do the tablecloth trick, even I admit I looked pretty guilty."

"Jason, you said that you followed someone outside the Welcome Center this morning," said Nancy. "Maybe that person is the suspect we're searching for. What did she look like?"

"I don't know. I only saw her from behind. It was a kid, so she must have been a camper."

"What color was her baseball cap?" asked George.

"She wasn't wearing one. She had long brown hair, but I saw a lot of campers in the Welcome Center with that same hairstyle."

"So there's no way to know what team she's on," Nancy said. This case really was a challenging one.

"Can you remember anything else that might

help us figure out who she is?" asked Bess.

"Not really, but I'll think about it," Jason promised, before hurrying ahead to catch up with the rest of the group, who had stopped by a willow tree at the end of the trail.

"Welcome to Turkey Trench," Lauren said when the Bluebirds were all together again. "It's pretty swampy here, so watch your step."

"Oh, look," Tessa cooed, pointing at a small pond surrounded by stones. "I wonder if there are any frogs in there."

"I'm sure there are," Lauren replied.

"Where there are frogs, there are bugs. Maybe even dragonflies." Tessa grinned before skipping over puddles and rocks to check out the shallow pool.

"Why is this place called Turkey Trench?" asked Peter.

"Look over there and you'll see." Lauren pointed to a flock of about ten funny-looking birds with red wattles and snoods strolling slowly toward them. The wild turkeys spread out across the marsh, pecking at large leafy yellow-green plants.

Suddenly, Nancy got a whiff of something foul. "Does anyone else smell a skunk?" she asked, making a face.

"I do." Bess groaned.

"Me too," Jason called, covering the bottom of his face with his cloak.

"Pee-ew," said George, pinching her nose.

"Don't worry, it's not a skunk," Lauren assured the campers.

"What is it, then?" asked George.

"I know! It's the turkeys' favorite snack." Peter pointed to one of the yellow-green plants.

"Turkeys like to eat the hard seeds that grow in the center. That's why they're pecking at them. And yes, the leaves smell like skunks. That's why the plants are called skunk cabbage."

Just then, a black-and-orange butterfly dipped and danced in the air above Tessa's head. "Look! It's a monarch," she cried, before tramping across the marsh, stepping on the skunk cabbage as she gave chase. The air filled with squawks and flapping as the startled turkeys took flight. By the time the butterfly flitted out of sight, Tessa was ankle-deep in the mucky pond, her tennis shoes covered in mud.

"Tessa, you chased the turkeys off," Peter complained, looking annoyed.

"Sorry," she said. "I got carried away and wasn't watching where I was going."

"Try to be more careful in the future," Lauren said gently. "This is where the turkeys live. We need to respect their habitat."

"I'll try," Tessa promised, before carefully stepping out of the shallow pool.

"Bluebirds, I see some woodpecker markings over there on the side of an oak tree," Lauren said. "Let's go check them out."

Peter and Tessa followed the counselor, but Jason hung back, motioning Nancy, George, and Bess over. "I need to talk to you," he said. "I remembered something about the girl I saw leaving the Welcome Center this morning. Tessa reminded me just now."

"What is it?" asked Nancy.

"She wasn't walking in a straight line. She kind of skipped back and forth, like Tessa did when she was chasing the butterfly. It was like the girl wasn't paying attention to where she was going."

"What else do you remember?" asked Bess.

"Not much," Jason replied with a shrug. "Only that when she got to the front door of the greenhouse, it didn't open."

George frowned. "So she didn't go inside?"

"She had a key in her pocket, and she used it to open the door, but I didn't wait around to see if she went in. I ran back to the Welcome Center to find Peter. I figured he'd be looking for me."

"She had a key?" Nancy couldn't believe her ears. "What is a camper doing with a key to the greenhouse?"

"No idea," Jason said.

"Hey, everyone!" Lauren called. "Is everything all right over there? You should join us. You're missing some great bird sightings."

"We just found some owl pellets!" yelled Peter.

"What's an owl pellet?" Jason asked.

"Owl puke!"

"Cool! I'm coming," Jason called, then dashed off.

As the Clue Crew walked slowly toward the rest of the group, Nancy opened the Clue Book and made some notes. "According to Jason, the girl who had a key to the greenhouse wasn't wearing a baseball cap."

"And she didn't have a swag bag, either," Bess remarked. "That's probably why the fake snake wound up in *my* bag." Nancy scribbled that down too.

"Maybe she wasn't a camper," George suggested.

"And from what Jason said, it seems like she was following something—maybe a butterfly—down the path toward the greenhouse," added Nancy.

Bess raised an eyebrow. "This is all starting to remind me of someone we know." She tilted her head in Tessa's direction.

Nancy closed the Clue Book and slipped it

back into her pocket. "We need to find out if Tessa has a key to the greenhouse."

"Are you saying the key might unlock this mystery?" George asked, doubling over at her own joke.

"Ooh, good one!" Nancy grinned. "That's exactly what I'm saying. Let's catch up to her and see what we can find out."

Chapter

BUG LOVE

"There's something I don't understand," said Bess as the girls made their way to where Tessa was standing by a blueberry bush. "Tessa's grandfather is in charge of taking care of those plants. Why would she destroy them?"

"I felt bad for Tessa when Dr. Giblet brought her to join our group," George added. "She was so upset her grandpa canceled their hike that she was crying."

"You mean that's why you *think* she was

crying," Bess argued. "We don't really know the reason."

George didn't want to admit it, but her cousin had a good point. "And that still doesn't explain why she would do something so awful."

"Maybe she figured if she ruined the plants her grandpa has to take care of, he'd have more time to spend with her," suggested Nancy.

"I guess that makes sense," Bess said after a moment, "but why would she steal the PowerTron 5000s?"

"She loves butterfly-watching as much as Jason loves jokes and Peter loves birds," George replied. "Maybe she took the binoculars to use on her butterfly hike with her grandpa?"

"And since Mr. Hebert is the head grounds-keeper, he would have a key to the greenhouse. Do you think Tessa took it?" Nancy asked.

"It's possible," admitted Bess. "Tessa seems so nice, though. She loves flowers and butterflies and frogs. She doesn't seem like the type of person who would do something so terrible."

Nancy wanted to ask Tessa about the key, but just as she was about to, a fat bumblebee zoomed past. Without watching where she was going, Tessa started following it as it buzzed through the air on its way to a sweet azalea bush. She tripped over a rock and fell, flattening a head of skunk cabbage. "Oops!" she said as she picked herself up.

"Not again!" muttered Peter.

"That girl could use a magic carpet," said Jason. "It would keep her from clomping all over the place."

Lauren shook her head, even though she had a small smile on her face. "Please try to be more careful, Tessa."

"Sorry!" Tessa called back.

Bess yanked Nancy and George off to the side again. "Maybe Tessa knocked over the plants by mistake. She never seems to watch where she's going."

"But if it were an accident, Tessa could have told us that when Jason was in the hot seat in the greenhouse earlier," Nancy whispered back.

"Do you think she's hiding something?" asked Bess.

"Yes," George replied. "I think she's hiding the PowerTron 5000s."

But Nancy wasn't so sure. "I agree with Bess. Tessa doesn't seem like she'd hurt a flea, let alone a tableful of plants. Still, we should find out where she was this morning."

Nancy, Bess, and George skipped over stones and leaped over puddles to catch up with Tessa, who was still by the sweet azalea bush.

"Did you see the butterfly? And the bumble-bee?" she asked. "I love bugs."

"Can we ask you a question?" Nancy said.

"Sure. Ask me anything. I know everything there is to know about insects."

Bess shook her head. "That's not what we want to talk about."

"*Achoo!*" Tessa sniffled. "I must be allergic to these flowers." Her eyes looked red again, like she'd been crying. She reached in her pocket for a tissue. When she pulled it out, a shiny key fell to the ground.

"Is that what I think it is?" said Nancy.

"It's a key to the greenhouse," Tessa explained. "I was supposed to give it back, but I forgot."

"Why do you have it?" George asked.

"Dr. Giblet gave it to me. She sent me to the greenhouse to find my grandpa when my mom dropped me off."

Bess leaned in. "So you *were* at the greenhouse this morning?"

"Yes, but—" Tessa's eyes went wide. "You don't think I'm the one who—"

"You know, Jason said he saw someone who looked like you open the greenhouse door with a key before camp this morning."

Tessa blew her nose again, folded the tissue, and dabbed her teary eyes. "That could have been me. Mom and I were already on our way to the park when Grandpa called to cancel our butterfly hike because he had so much work to do to get ready for the Big Bird Count." She inspected the tissue for a dry spot, but the wad was damp and shredded. "Grandpa told my mom to drop me off anyway. He thought it would still be fun for me to spend the day with a group of campers."

"But that doesn't explain what you were doing at the greenhouse and why you have a key."

"Dr. Giblet said I could say a quick hello to Grandpa before she brought me to meet up with Team Bluebird. She gave me a key so I could leave a note for him in case—in case—*Achoo!*"

"Bless you," said Nancy. "Boy, you really are allergic to those flowers, aren't you?"

"I am." Tessa wiped her nose, then sneezed again.

Bess dug into her bag, then handed Tessa a fresh tissue from a small pack she'd stashed there earlier. George rolled her eyes. "Of course you have tissues with you."

"What? You know I like to be prepared for all possible emergencies."

"I know, I know. But who expects to meet someone allergic to the outdoors at a nature park?"

"Oh, I don't let my allergies keep me indoors," Tessa insisted. "I took an allergy pill in the car. It took a while to kick in, but I felt a lot better—that is, until I got too close to these white flowers."

"So this morning when you joined our group, you weren't crying because your grandpa canceled your butterfly hike?" George asked.

"Nope. I wasn't sad at all. I know Grandpa will make it up to me. We hike together all the time. *Achoo!*"

Bess handed Tessa the whole pack of tissues. "Keep them. You need them more than I do."

"Thank you." Tessa sniffled.

"Let's get you away from this bush," said Nancy, leading the girls back toward Lauren, Jason, and Peter. She was careful not to step in marshy mud puddles. "You were about to say something just now, before you sneezed."

"Oh, that's right. Dr. Giblet gave me a key to the greenhouse so I could leave a note for Grandpa in case he wasn't there."

"And was he? There, I mean?" asked George.

"Yeah. That's why I didn't go inside."

Following Tessa's line of thinking is like watching a crow fly, Nancy thought. *It's never in a straight line.* "If your grandpa was there, why didn't you go in?"

"Once I opened the door, I saw Grandpa talking to someone," Tessa explained. "It looked like a serious conversation, and I didn't want to interrupt."

"Do you know who he was talking to?" asked Bess.

"I'm not sure. A lady. She reminded me of someone, but I can't remember who . . ." Tessa tapped her temple, like she was thinking hard. "Nope, it's not coming to me."

"Do you remember what the woman said?" asked Nancy.

"Something about a secret. She hoped Hazel wouldn't find out."

"Hazel?" Nancy said. "That's Dr. Giblet's first name."

"But why would the mystery woman want to keep a secret from the park director?" asked Bess.

"I don't know." Tessa shrugged. "I didn't stick around. I wanted to get back to chasing the butterfly."

"Hey, Tessa!" Lauren called. "I spotted a beautiful dragonfly I think you'll like. Come see!"

"Really?" With that, Tessa dashed off, leaving Nancy and her friends to figure out their next steps.

"So it seems the break-in bandit isn't Jason or Tessa," Nancy said, taking out the Clue Book and crossing Tessa's name off her list.

"But now we have a new suspect!" Bess replied, bouncing on her toes. "We need to find out who this mystery lady with her mystery secret is."

George grinned. "I guess that means the case of the Bird Bonanza Break-in is still *up in the air.*"

"That's a good one, George," Bess said with a giggle.

"It is a funny joke," Nancy agreed. "I just wish it weren't so true."

Chapter

7

LUNCH HUNCH

"Look up there," Lauren instructed, pointing to a branch. "There's a young hawk high up in that hemlock tree."

"I see it," said Bess. "It's got tan and white feathers."

"You'll get a better view with these," Lauren replied, handing Bess her binoculars.

Bess took a look and

passed them to George. "Are these as good as the PowerTron 5000s?" George asked.

Lauren laughed. "They're not even close. The PowerTron 5000s are much stronger, but mine are fine for seeing birds that aren't too far away."

Peter, Jason, and Tessa each took a turn with the binoculars, then Tessa handed them to Nancy.

When Nancy peered through the lenses, she saw the hawk spread its wings and take off. It flew across the marsh before settling in a pine tree. Beneath the tree a woman was crouching on the ground, surrounded by the flock of turkeys. She looked exactly like Dr. Giblet, but this woman was wearing regular outdoor clothes instead of a nature park uniform. Next to her on the ground, Nancy saw a wide-brimmed hat. Nancy realized this was the woman she had bumped into at the Welcome Center! She watched as the woman stood up, brushed off her shorts, and put on her hat before she headed deeper into the woods and out of sight.

"Oops! I lost track of time," Lauren said, interrupting Nancy's thoughts. "We'd better head back for lunch."

"Good! I'm starving!" said Jason.

"Me too," said Bess.

Lauren checked her watch. "We'd better hustle. We're running late."

As they walked back toward the Welcome Center, Lauren and Peter pointed out different types of birds and taught the campers their names. Soon enough, the Bluebirds arrived at the picnic area next to the Welcome Center. The other teams were already at their tables gobbling up lunch.

"Here's a good spot," Lauren said, motioning to an empty table under a tall birch.

"I'll be right back," said Tessa. "Dr. Giblet is keeping my lunch in the refrigerator inside."

"Does anyone remember the names of any of the birds we saw today?" Lauren asked as the campers dug into their sandwiches.

"Um, we saw a goldfinch," George said through a mouthful of egg salad.

Nancy snapped her fingers as she tried to remember the name of the dark little bird with the speckled feathers. "And a starling!"

"And my favorite—a dark-eyed junco," added Bess.

Tessa slid onto the bench next to George with her lunch bag. She giggled. "Dark-eyed junco. That's a funny name."

"Oh, you don't know the half of it," Peter replied with a chuckle. "Lots of birds have really strange names. Ever heard of a smew?"

"A *smew*? What kind of bird is that?" asked Bess.

Peter grinned. "It's a black-and-white duck. They don't live around here, though, so we probably won't see one, right, Lauren?"

"That's right. Smews live mostly in Europe and Asia."

The table was quiet as the campers munched on their sandwiches. "Peter, will you tell us more silly bird names?" Tessa asked after a moment.

Peter wiped his mouth with a napkin. "Well, there's the tropical boubou."

George almost spit out her lemonade. "A bou-bou? That bird sounds like it needs a bandage."

"You won't see that one around here either," Lauren said. "Tropical boubous live in Africa."

Tessa slurped the last drops of fruit punch from her juice pouch. "All the cool birds seem to live far away."

"Eagles live around here," said Peter. "I'd really like to see one."

Lauren gave him a smile. "Keep your eyes on the skies and I'm sure you will eventually."

Jason pulled at the cape strings tied under his chin. "Are there any birds that do tricks?" he asked.

"Actually, there *is* a bird that's tricky, but in a mean way—not like the funny pranks you pull," Peter replied. "It's called a brown-headed cow-bird."

Tessa chuckled. "A cowbird? That's another funny name!"

"Does it look like a cow?" Nancy asked.

"No," Peter answered, scratching his head.

"Actually, I'm not sure why they call it a cowbird. Do you know, Lauren?"

"They get their name from where they live, near grazing cows. Where there are cows, there are lots of delicious bugs to eat."

"I love bugs too," said Tessa. "Maybe I'm like a cowbird."

Peter shook his head. "I hope not. Cowbirds are stinkers."

"What do they do?" asked Nancy.

"They lay their eggs in other birds' nests. The other bird parents can't tell the difference, so they get fooled into raising chicks that aren't their own."

Bess gasped. "That's terrible!"

"You're right. I would never play a mean prank like that," Jason said with a frown.

"The other birds don't seem to mind," Peter added. "They raise the cowbird chicks along with their own families."

"But the cowbird chick is still an impostor," George insisted before tipping her thermos and letting the last few drips of lemonade land on her tongue.

"What's an impostor?" asked Tessa.

"Someone who pretends to be somebody else," Bess explained.

"It usually means that the person is up to no good," added George.

"That's *it*!" cried Nancy, jumping up.

George nearly toppled off the bench. "What? What did I say?"

"There's an impostor here at camp pretending to be Dr. Giblet," said Nancy. "I bumped into her this morning, and I saw her again through the binoculars at Turkey Trench. I'm willing to bet that it's the same person Tessa saw talking to her grandpa about keeping a secret from Dr. Giblet. Didn't you say the lady you saw reminded you of someone?"

"That's right!" Tessa said, holding up a finger. "The lady did look like Dr. Giblet."

Nancy's eyes narrowed. "George and Bess, help me clear the table?"

George groaned. "Aww, do we have to? Oww!"

Bess had shoved an elbow into her cousin's ribs, then made her eyes go wide.

"Oh!" George said, giving her cousin a knowing nod.

"We'll carry these to the trash bin," Nancy called over her shoulder.

"Be right back," Bess added. George reached for a crumpled napkin before she slipped off the bench and rushed to follow them.

"That's very nice of you girls," Lauren said as the Clue Crew darted off.

After they dumped the trash in the bin, Bess squirted everyone's hands with sanitizer she had in her pocket. This time, George was glad her cousin was always super prepared.

Nancy whipped out the Clue Book. "We don't have much time. Let's brainstorm quickly."

"I have more of a question than a clue," said George. "Why would anyone pretend to be Dr. Giblet?"

"Dr. Giblet is in charge of the whole park. Someone who looks and acts like her could get away with anything," Bess said, tapping her lip. "Like sneaking into the greenhouse."

"Or stealing a pair of PowerTron 5000s," George added.

"So do we have a new suspect?" Nancy asked her friends.

"Sort of," Bess answered. "We know what this mystery lady looks like, but don't know who she is."

Nancy flipped to the page in her notebook where she'd written Jason's and Tessa's names, then crossed them out. At the bottom of the list, she wrote IMPOSTOR.

Bess frowned. "We'd better get to the bottom of this soon."

"But how?" George asked.

Nancy shut the notebook with determined *thwack*! "We'll find a way. We always do."

Chapter

8

POSSIBLE IMPOSTOR

The rest of the Bluebirds had already stashed their lunch coolers in their swag bags when Nancy, George, and Bess returned to the table.

Lauren twirled the cover of her thermos closed. "You three looked like you were having a serious conversation over by the trash bin just now. Is everything okay? Remember, I am your Bird Bonanza Camp counselor, and I'm here to help."

"Actually, we weren't talking about birds," George admitted.

Bess tugged at the bird whistle around her neck. "We think we might have a new suspect in the greenhouse case."

"And the first thing we need to do is tell Dr. Giblet that there's someone at camp pretending to be her," Nancy said. "Then we should track down Mr. Hebert to ask him about the 'secret' he and the impostor are keeping together."

"My grandpa wouldn't do anything wrong," Tessa insisted.

Nancy smiled at her new friend. "But he might know who would."

Lauren shook her head gently. "I love your enthusiasm, girls, but remember, you're here as campers, not detectives."

Nancy shot George and Bess a knowing look. No matter what, if there was a mystery to solve, the Clue Crew would be on the case.

Lauren checked her clipboard. "I hope you can direct that excitement into building bird feeders. Next up we have arts and crafts in the Welcome Center."

George bounced in her seat. "With power tools? Like a table saw?"

"That's the spirit!" Lauren's eyes twinkled. "Actually, the pieces are already cut, but they do need to be put together. Would a hammer and nails tempt you? And pots full of paint?"

"Definitely!" said George. Bess rolled her eyes and shot Nancy a look. George loved tools and gadgets, but they all enjoyed arts and crafts projects. Nancy thought building bird feeders together might give them time to think more about their clues.

"Is there purple paint?" Tessa asked as the Bluebirds walked back into the Welcome Center and Lauren led them down a hall toward the arts and crafts room. "Purple is my favorite color."

"Look, there's her office," Nancy whispered to her friends. She pointed to a wooden door with a nameplate: DR. HAZEL GIBLET, PARK DIRECTOR. The door was closed, but they could see through a small window that a light was on inside.

"Maybe we could take a quick break during

the building workshop to go see her," George whispered back.

"Good thinking," Bess said.

The kids on Team Chickadee and Team Robin, who had finished lunch early, were already at their tables banging away when the Bluebirds entered the art room. "We're over here by the window," Lauren called to her campers over the noise. Birdfeeder kits with wooden pieces and a list of instructions waited for them on a round table by the sink.

"It's really loud in here," said Peter as he emptied his kit onto the table and inspected the pieces, arranging them like a jigsaw puzzle into the shape of a birdfeeder.

"And we're about to make it even louder," Jason replied. "I'm going to the workbench to grab a hammer." He headed across the room toward the tool table.

"Get me one too!" Peter called.

"Me too!" said Tessa.

"Me three!" added George with a grin. Jason

returned with enough tools for everyone, and the gang set to work building.

Lauren circled the table. "Let me know if you need a hand."

The group was quiet, thanks to all the banging, but once her birdfeeder was assembled, Nancy was eager to get away with George and Bess to discuss the case. As she dabbed her feeder with blue paint, she noticed that George and Bess were almost finished too. She was relieved to see that Peter, Jason, and Tessa still had a little more to do.

"Lauren, would it be okay if Bess, George, and I went to Dr. Giblet's office? We want to tell her about the lady who looks like her and ask her if she knows anything else about the greenhouse break-in."

"It's only a few feet away down the hall," Bess said.

"We won't be gone long," added George.

"You three sure are determined detectives, aren't you?" Lauren sighed. "Yes, you can go. Stay together, though, and be back in five minutes. We have to move on to our next activity soon."

Tessa dropped her purple paintbrush.

"Hey! You splattered my birdfeeder," Jason complained.

"Sorry!"

"Don't worry," Peter said. "You can paint over it." He handed his brother the pot of red paint.

Nancy grabbed Bess and George by their elbows and walked quickly to the door. "We'll rush back! We promise!"

Nancy knocked on Dr. Giblet's door, but there was no answer. She tried the knob and was

surprised when it turned and the door squeaked as it opened. "Dr. Giblet? Are you in here?" There was no response.

"Should we go in?" asked George.

"Of course not," Bess replied. "You know better than that, George Fayne!"

"We could pop in to leave a note on her desk,"

Nancy suggested. "We'll tell her we need to see her as soon as possible. That should be okay, right?"

"I guess so," said Bess, but she didn't look convinced.

Inside the office was a large desk. On the wall behind it, a tall bookshelf held books about birds, natural history, animals, insects, freshwater fish, and other subjects. A glass cabinet on the opposite wall displayed collections of bird feathers, snail shells, and pressed leaves and flowers, along with several photographs.

George sidled up to the cabinet to look at the colorful feather collection. "This place is so cool."

"Don't touch anything," Bess scolded. "We're only here to leave Dr. Giblet a note."

"I would never," George shot back.

"Hey, look at this," Nancy said, pointing at a notepad sitting in the middle of the desk. The girls gathered around to get a closer look:

1. Cancel Big Bird Count.

2. Call Mabel.

"Who's Mabel?" Bess wondered aloud.

"And does this note mean that the Big Bird Count is definitely canceled?" George asked, frowning.

Just then, the girls heard voices—a man's and a woman's—outside Dr. Giblet's office door.

"Did you take care of our little secret?" the woman asked. Quickly, Nancy, Bess, and George squished themselves underneath the desk.

"Why are we hiding?" George whispered.

"It's a secret," Nancy hissed back.

George made a face. "Why can't you just tell me?"

"It's *their* secret!" Nancy put her finger up to her lips. "Listen."

The pair entered Dr. Giblet's office. "I took care of my part of the plan," the woman said. "Now it's your turn."

"Hazel will be back soon. Let's get the photograph and get out of here before anyone sees us," said the man. Nancy recognized his voice. It was Mr. Hebert!

"Great," the woman said. "Then I can get back to the greenhouse to finish the job."

The girls heard the glass cabinet door click open, then heard it shut again a few moments later. "I've got it," said Mr. Hebert. "Hurry, let's go."

As the pair was about to leave, Nancy heard a third voice—Lauren's. "Hello, Mr. Hebert and Dr. Marsh. Have you seen any of my Bluebirds? I'm missing three of them. They came in here to find Dr. Giblet."

"What should we do?" George hissed.

"We have to tell Lauren we're under here," Bess whispered miserably. "We were supposed to be quick."

"Um, we're under here," Nancy called out as the girls spilled from underneath the desk.

"What were you doing under there?" Lauren asked.

"That's a very good question," said Mr. Hebert. "Were you spying on us?" Next to him stood the Dr. Giblet look-alike, the woman Lauren had called Dr. Marsh.

Before Nancy could respond, Dr. Giblet

pushed through the crowd into her office. "What are you all doing in here?" she asked.

"We were looking for you," replied Nancy.

"And *we* were looking for *you*," Lauren said to Nancy, Bess, and George. "You girls said that you'd be right back. I left the rest of the Bluebirds with one of the other counselors while they finished cleaning up their workspaces. We're running behind again."

"Dr. Giblet wasn't here when we knocked," Nancy explained, "so we were leaving her a note."

"What is it that you needed to tell me?" Dr. Giblet asked.

Just then, Peter, Jason, and Tessa poked their heads into the office. "We're finished cleaning up, and our bird feeders are drying by the open window," Peter announced, not realizing he'd interrupted.

"Grandpa!" cried Tessa, running into Mr. Hebert's arms. "I can't wait to show you my bird feeder. It's *purple*."

"Your favorite color." Mr. Hebert smiled.

"Mr. Hebert, Mabel, is there a reason you're in my office? Did you need to speak to me as well?"

"Um, not exactly . . . ," said Dr. Marsh. Her eyes shifted around the room and her cheeks turned pink.

"Well, then, what's going on here?" Dr. Giblet demanded, putting her hands on her hips.

Nancy couldn't stay quiet another minute. "Bess, George, and I are the Clue Crew. We solve mysteries. And we think we know who broke into the greenhouse!"

"Tell me," said Dr. Giblet.

"It was your impostor," said Nancy, tilting her head toward the woman who looked like Dr. Giblet. "She told Mr. Hebert that she's keeping a secret from you. And just now she said that she was headed back to the greenhouse to 'finish the job.'"

"I'm sure my grandpa had nothing to do with whatever's going on," Tessa insisted. "He wouldn't do anything to cause trouble."

"Of course he wouldn't," said Dr. Marsh, smiling kindly at Nancy and her friends.

"And that's no impostor," said Dr. Giblet. "That's my cousin, Dr. Mabel Marsh."

"Dr. M-Mabel M-Marsh!" Peter stammered. "You're no burglar. You're famous! I can't believe I'm meeting you! You're my hero!"

Chapter

9

BIRDS OF A FEATHER

"I'm very pleased to meet you, Peter," Dr. Marsh said once Lauren had introduced them. "Are you interested in birds?"

"Is he *ever*!" Jason blurted out. "My brother is obsessed with birds."

"I want to be an ornithologist like you when I grow up," Peter added once he'd found his voice again.

"Do you have a favorite bird?" Dr. Marsh asked.

"I love eagles, but I've never actually seen one in real life."

"Keep up with your interest in bird science, and I'm sure you'll see an eagle one day," she said.

"Peter is your biggest fan," Jason told Dr. Marsh. "He keeps checking your book *Talking Turkey* out of the library."

"My dad and I read it together," Peter said, blushing. "He loves birds too."

"Then I hope you enjoy my new book, *Birds of a Feather*. It's about how turkeys travel in family groups. I was going to discuss it during my presentation on Big Bird Count Day."

"I was about to call you. I'm afraid I have to cancel the Big Bird Count," said Dr. Giblet with a big sigh.

"Oh no," Dr. Marsh replied. "Mr. Hebert was telling me about the greenhouse break-in, but do you really have to cancel? That would be such a shame."

"It wouldn't be fair to hold the event if we can't offer the raffle prize," Dr. Giblet explained.

"True birders care about the birds," Dr. Marsh countered. "Maybe you don't need a prize."

"That's what I said," Peter insisted. "The count is about making sure the birds have a safe place to live. That's the important thing."

"True," said Dr. Giblet. "But until we know who or what broke into the greenhouse, stole the prize binoculars, and ruined all the plants, I'm not sure it's safe to invite so many visitors to the park."

"I see your point," said Dr. Marsh, nodding. "Still, it's a pity."

Dr. Giblet grew quiet for a moment, then looked puzzled. "I know you didn't break into the greenhouse, Mabel," she said, "but why did these young detectives suspect you? And why were you in my office?"

Dr. Marsh and Mr. Hebert shared a knowing look. "We *are* keeping a secret from you, but it has nothing to do with today's unfortunate events."

Mr. Hebert held up the picture that he had taken from the glass cabinet. It was a photograph of Dr. Marsh and Dr. Giblet posing in front of a waterfall.

"Oh, I love this picture," said Dr. Giblet. "That was a bird-watching trip Mabel and I took together. We saw rare loons that day."

"I wanted the picture so I could frame it for you. In fact, I have a few gifts I wanted to give you to thank you for being such a special friend and cousin. I was going to keep them a secret until my presentation on Big Bird Count Day, but if the event's canceled, I might as well share them with you now."

Dr. Marsh pulled a book out from her bag and handed it to Dr. Giblet. It had a picture of a flock of turkeys on the cover. "Look at the front. I dedicated my new book to you."

Dr. Giblet opened to the first page and read aloud, "'To my dear cousin, Hazel. Birds of a feather flock together. We are of a feather, and I couldn't ask for a better cousin or friend. Love, Mabel.'" Tears filled Dr. Giblet's eyes as she pulled Dr. Marsh into a tight hug. "Thank you."

"I have something else for you in the

greenhouse—a potted bee balm plant. I was just headed over there to get it ready."

"Bee balm is my favorite flower," said Dr. Giblet. "Its pink spiky petals attract hummingbirds, which are my favorite birds."

"I was keeping it hidden in a corner of the greenhouse to help with the surprise," Mr. Hebert explained. "Don't worry. It wasn't one of the plants destroyed during the break-in."

"So that's what you were talking about when you said you were going to the greenhouse to 'finish the job'?" Nancy asked.

"That's right," replied Dr. Marsh. "I was going to make sure it was watered and put a pretty bow on it."

Nancy squinted, thinking hard, then her eyes shot open.

"I know that look," said Bess.

George grinned. "You have a hunch hatching, don't you?"

"I think so. I hope so. Dr. Giblet, did you say bee balm flowers attract hummingbirds?"

"Yes, that's right, like a magician attracts an audience." When she nodded in Jason's direction, he blushed and smiled back.

"All the plants in the greenhouse have something that birds like—tasty leaves or sweet-smelling nectar," Mr. Hebert added. "That's what makes them bird-friendly."

"But birds aren't the only animals that love those kinds of foods," Nancy noted. "Mr. Hebert, you keep seeds in the greenhouse, right?"

"Of course. The seed packets are in a wooden box on a shelf near my workbench."

"On the shelf right above where the PowerTron 5000s were stored?"

"That's right."

"We saw the seeds this morning," said Bess. She tugged at the bird whistle around her neck. "But seeds belong in a greenhouse, so we didn't think they were an important clue."

"The packets were all ripped up," Tessa reminded the group.

"I thought that was because Mr. Hebert

opened the packets to plant the seeds," Nancy explained, "but maybe I was wrong."

"So you think it was something else?" asked George.

"I do. And if I'm right, we'd better get to the greenhouse fast before there's another break-in!"

Clue Crew—and YOU!

Can you solve the case of the greenhouse break-in before the culprit flies the coop? Try thinking like the Clue Crew. Write your answers down on a separate piece of paper or turn the page.

1. Nancy, Bess, and George are sure that Jason, Tessa, and Dr. Marsh aren't responsible for the greenhouse mess. Can you think of someone else who might have wanted to ruin the plants and take the PowerTron 5000s?

2. At first, the Clue Crew didn't think anything was out of place in the greenhouse, but then they remembered the ripped-up seed packets. Are there any other clues they could use to solve the case?

3. At Bird Bonanza Camp, the Bluebirds learn about some of nature's magic tricks. Can you think of any others? Would one of them help with the solution to this mystery?

Chapter

EAGLE EYE

Together, the group exited Dr. Giblet's office and the Welcome Center. Nancy led the others down the short path to the greenhouse, where Mr. Hebert unlocked the front door.

"We're too late!" cried Dr. Giblet. Broken pots and smashed flowers were strewn across the floor.

Lauren groaned. "Not again."

"Look! There!" Nancy called, pointing to the ceiling. A pair of gray squirrels twitched and squeaked, rolling over each other on the ledge. In their scuffling, one of them kicked over a flower-pot full of dirt, sending it crashing to the floor. Startled, the pair scrambled away and disappeared through the small window in the roof.

"Squirrels? Squirrels are responsible? I can't believe it," said Dr. Giblet.

Mr. Hebert moved a step stool beneath the window and climbed up to inspect where the squirrels had escaped. "I see what happened. They came through the ventilation window."

"Is that what that window is for? Ventilation?" asked George.

"That's right," Mr. Hebert replied. "The plants need warmth to grow, but they also need fresh air. There's usually a screen fastened over the opening, but it looks like the squirrels ripped a hole in it."

"That explains the mess in here," said Lauren, spreading her arms wide.

"We still don't know what happened to the PowerTron 5000s, though," said George.

"I'll bet Nancy has a clue," Bess suggested.

"I do." Nancy walked over to where the

binoculars had been stored. On the shelf above, she found the wooden box containing Mr. Hebert's shredded seed packets.

"I remembered how much the squirrels loved the seeds and oranges Lauren put in the bird feeders. I'll bet seeds in a greenhouse are just as tasty."

She pointed to the empty bag of soil on the ground next to the flowerpot. "When the squirrels came looking for the seeds, they must have knocked this bag upside down, and the dirt spilled in here." She knelt to inspect the pot, then plunged her hands in up to her elbows.

"Nancy, what are you doing? You're going to be a mess," Bess cried.

"Worth it," George said, as she darted over to help Nancy dig. Together, the girls pulled a box out from under the soil.

"Ta-da!" George crowed. "Here they are." She lifted a box labeled POWERTRON 5000 above her head.

"Thank goodness they're still in their original packaging," said Dr. Giblet. "No dirt got inside to ruin them."

"The squirrels must have knocked the binoculars into the empty flowerpot when they were stealing the seeds from Mr. Hebert's seed packets," said Lauren.

"And then knocked the soil over on top of them," Dr. Marsh added.

"That's some trick," said Jason. "I'm impressed."

Nancy dusted off her hands. "I'm just happy we solved the mystery."

"Does this mean the Big Bird Count is back on?" asked Peter.

"It sure does." Dr. Giblet smiled. "Thanks to you, Clue Crew."

"And the winner of the PowerTron 5000s is"—Dr. Giblet unfolded the piece of paper she'd pulled from the raffle hat—"Team Bluebird's Georgia Fayne!"

"That's you!" squealed Bess.

"Don't remind me," George groaned. "I hate it when people call me by my real name."

"You're not going to let that keep you from claiming your prize, are you?" Nancy teased.

"No way!" George skipped up to the front of the picnic area to collect the binoculars from Dr. Giblet. She was smiling from ear to ear when she returned to the table.

"Good for you, George." Lauren grinned. "You helped solve the mystery and find the PowerTron 5000s. I'm glad your name was the lucky pick."

"Thank you for teaching me all those bird names," George said, then turned to Peter. "And thank you for letting me tag along with you during the count."

"It was fun doing the Big Bird Count with you," Peter said.

"Are you saying you're glad I didn't do the count with you?" Jason asked, pouting.

"Sitting out of the count gave you extra time to practice the tablecloth trick," Peter reminded his brother. "You're a master at it now!" He held out his fist. Jason gave him a gentle bump and they wiggled their fingers.

George noticed Peter was hugging a book

to his chest with his other arm. "Isn't that Dr. Marsh's new book?"

"Yeah. She gave me a copy after her presentation. She autographed it, too. Wanna see?"

"Yes," said George. Peter handed her the book.

To my new friend, Peter. Always look to the skies. That's where you'll find your prize. Happy birding! Dr. Mabel Marsh

"That's really nice," said Bess.

George unwrapped her new binoculars. "Do you want to be the first to try them out, Peter?" she asked.

"Sure." He took them and peered through the lenses up at the sky. "Wait, you won't believe this, but I think that's a . . . that's a . . ."

"That's a what?" asked Nancy.

"Spit it out," said Jason.

"That's an *eagle!*" He watched as the grand bird dipped and swooped in circles overhead. After it flew away, he handed the binoculars back to George and smiled. "Dr. Marsh was right. My prize was in the skies!"

"Hey, Bluebirds!" Tessa called, approaching their table with Mr. Hebert at her side.

"Hi, Tessa," Peter replied. "You missed the Big Bird Count. Where have you been?"

"Grandpa and I just got back from our butterfly hike. I didn't count birds, but I saw twenty-five different types of moths and butterflies today. That's a record for us, isn't it, Grandpa?"

"It sure is." Mr. Hebert smiled.

"I can't believe Bird Bonanza Camp is over," said Bess. "I had so much fun."

"Solving mysteries makes everything more fun," Nancy reminded her friends.

"Even I had a good time," Jason said. Today, he

was wearing a regular T-shirt, shorts, and sneakers instead of his magician gear. His bird whistle hung around his neck.

"I could ask Mom if we could do another week at nature camp," Peter suggested.

"Or we could go to magician camp," Jason replied hopefully.

"Let's toss a coin. Whoever wins gets to decide," Peter offered. He pulled a penny from his pocket and tossed it in the air.

"Heads!" called Jason.

Peter lifted his hand to take a peek when the coin landed. Nancy looked over his shoulder. She could see that the coin had landed on tails. "Heads it is. I guess we're going to magician camp next after all." Peter gave Nancy a wink.

"Yes!" Jason exclaimed, flapping his arms like wings in a happy dance.

Nancy giggled. "I had a feeling that was going to happen."

"How did you know?" asked Bess.

"Let's just say a little birdie told me!"